FORBIDDEN TO TELL

SHANNON SPRUILL

SMS Write One Publishing, LLC
Cheektowaga, New York

SMS Write On Publishing
3843 Union Road
Suite 15 #141
Cheektowaga, NY 14225

Publisher's Note: This is a work of fiction. Names, characters, places, and incidents are a product of the author's imagination. Locales and public names are sometimes used for atmospheric purposes. Any resemblance to actual people, living or dead, or to businesses, companies, events, institutions, or locales is completely coincidental.

Book Layout ©2017 BookDesignTemplates.com

Forbidden To Tell/ Shannon Spruill. -- 1st ed.
ISBN 978-0-692-85121-0

Contents

I can do all things through Christ which strengtheneth me.

–Philippians 4:13 (King James Bible)

****

ONE

MEET THE MATTHEWS

As I laid there looking up at the ceiling my only thought was, "when will this be over?" This massive body lying on top of me with sweat dripping and I would occasionally let out a fake moan of pleasure and this made him go harder. Panting and sweating, faster and faster as he went deeper inside of me until finally he was spent. He rolled from on top of me with a smile on his face. "Was it good for you baby?" I smiled and said, "oh yes it was good." I turned on my side and as soon as I heard him snoring I began to cry. I loved my husband but hated when he touched me. I found no pleasure in our intimacy. I would be happy if we were never intimate.

David was a successful graphic designer and I was a social worker with the Nassau County child protective services. Our tagline for Nassau county CPS was "It shouldn't hurt to be a child." After we got married in June 2012, we moved to Hempstead, Long Island. We owned a 4-bedroom ranch in a quiet tree line neighborhood. We had no children because we were both focused on our careers but I knew that eventually David wanted children. I did not want children. Why? I was not quite sure why or I never took time to look deeper into my feelings or maybe I just did not want to know why. The next morning David was up early and in the kitchen cooking breakfast. Yes, I had a husband who loved to cook. While he was making breakfast, I took a shower. I walked into the kitchen to the smell of bacon, sausage, and French toast. "Do you want some apple juice or hot chocolate?" He was so thoughtful. "I will have apple juice." It was a beautiful Sunday morning and I

FORBIDDEN TO TELL

knew what was next. David was big about spending our Sunday's together. Because we both had very busy work lives, Sunday was dedicated to us. "What do you want to get into today?" David had the sexiest eyes and it was difficult to deny him. "David, I am sorry but today, I have a very important case that I must follow up on. I know Sundays are ours but I will definitely make it up to you, I promise." He dropped his lip and hung his head. "Don't make me feel bad." He started laughing, "Don't worry, it's cool. I will make you a delicious dinner tonight. I going to run down to the gym and I will see you later." He planted a kiss on my lips and left. I hated lying to David but there were some things that he would never understand. There were some things I didn't understand.

TWO

****

FELIX

I sat in my car feeling like a detective on a stake out. I watched as my mother pulled up to the parking lot of The Regency Assisted Living Facility. She went in and then I got out of my car and followed her at a safe distant so she would not see me. She stopped at the front desk and was pointed to a door that led to the outside garden. She walked over to where Felix was sitting. They sat and talked for about 30 minutes. She brought him a sandwich and they ate lunch together. I just looked at him with such hate. He was suffering from Alzheimer and probably would not even remember who I was, but I could not find it in my heart to have pity on him. He was very frail. He could not have been more than 150 lbs. soak and wet. A mere shell of the man I remembered. I would often follow my mother here and sit in the distance and watch. But today was going to be different. I waited for my mother to leave. I walked over to where Felix was sitting. I walked up to him and looked him in his eyes. His eyes were blank. He had no idea who I was and he just looked at me with no emotion. Why was I torturing myself? How was I going to make him understand what he had done and how he ruined my life? The point of all of this was to show him but if he did not recognize me then what was the purpose? I turned to walk away and suddenly with a soft voice he said, "Roxanne." I froze where I stood. I turned and quickly grabbed him by the shoulders and said "You remember me, don't you? Answer me!" Once again there was that blank stare. I started to shake him, "You answer me! Answer me now!!" I saw a worker headed in my direction and yelling, "Miss, what are you doing? Stop!

Leave Mr. Felix alone!" I quickly turned and made my exit. I jumped in my car and sped away.

As I drove home, I could not help but think about Felix. Did he recognize me? Did he remember? He called my name and that had to mean he remembered something. But what did he remember. As I watched that feeble old man, I wondered was he physically suffering and what was he thinking about. There was a part of me that wanted him to suffer but there was also a part of me that felt sorry for him. I did not like feeling sorry for him. I got back home before David and I took a nice long, hot shower. I was glad I got home first, so I could find a reason to avoid his advances when he got home. I often wondered can you love someone without physical contact. I truly loved David and wanted to have a happy normal marriage but I was living a lie. I sat down on the side of the bed and pulled out my journal and wrote about my visit to see Felix. After I finished journaling, I went into my office and started looking over my case file for the following day. I had to investigate a family where a little girl had been showing up to school with bruises on her arms and legs. Family dynamics was a mother, stepfather, and daughter. The work I did was my way of trying to be a help to the many helpless children of abuse. I was passionate about my work because no child should have to endure any type of abuse. Being a child should be about innocence, fun and not worrying about the things adults had to worry about. David often told me that I get too personally involved in my work, but I knew no other way to do my job. I suspected the father was the abuser in this case and the mother knows what is going on. She is so caught up in this man that she is willing to risk the well-being of her child. This made me angry but I had to keep my emotions in check because I needed to be professional if I was going to be able to help this little girl. There were times that my job wore on me but I could not abandon these children. They needed someone who truly understood what they were going through. I truly understood. My thoughts went back to Felix. I was still struggling with feeling sorry for him and despising him. Suddenly the doorbell rang. I was not expecting anyone and I really was not in the mood for company. I quietly walked to the front door and I look through the peep hole and to my dismay it was my mother. I took a deep breath and wondered if I was very quiet, maybe she would leave. What could she possibly want? I just stood there and it seemed like I was standing there forever waiting to hear her footsteps as she left. Before she left, she slipped a note under the door and then I heard her footsteps as she left. I took a deep breath and let out a sigh of relief. I could not deal with her today. I picked up the note and begin to read it. "Roxanne, I stopped by today. I hope you are doing well and just wanted to let you know that I saw your father today. He barely remembers me but he is doing as well as can be expected. It might help if you visited him. I know you have your reasons but I thought I would mention it. Call me when you get a chance, Mom." I crumbled up the note and tossed it in the garbage. I hope she was not holding her breath for a phone call any time soon. I just did not have time for her drama at this point in my life. I am glad David was not home because I would have had to answer the door and make nice. Could you love and despise someone on that same time? I felt like I had an obligation to love my mother but I despised her and did not like her. So much of my torment today was her doing.

THREE

****

AMANDA

The following morning I was up before David could turn over for some morning nooky. I took a shower and I was downstairs making him breakfast. He came in the kitchen watching me with a curious smile. "Wow, what did I do to deserve all of this?" "Who said this was for you?" He came over and pulled me into his arms and kissed me so passionately. David knew how to make me feel so special and I wish I could give him one hundred percent of myself. I was making his favorite; ham and cheese omelet with grits and butter. I enjoyed seeing him smile and being pleased with me. "I have some errands to run after work and then I will be going to dinner with Crystal. Will you be ok for dinner tonight?" He dropped his bottom lip and began to pout and then flash a smile. "I will be fine. I am going to see dad tonight." "Give him my love. I am going to get ready to leave because I want to stop by the office before I go out into the field. I love you and call me later."

My drive to the office was only 10 minutes. My office was in Uniondale, New York. Today I did not turn on the car radio. When I had to make a home visit for one of my cases, I usually did not turn on the radio. I just thought about what I was headed into. What condition would I find the child? Was it just physical abuse or was sexual abuse also involved. The child's name was Amanda. Such a pretty name and a tragedy that anyone would raise their hand to strike this child or any child. This always made me mad but I had to keep it professional if I was going to help these children. My job was about helping the children that did not have the courage to speak out and let someone know what was happening to them. When you walk into my office building the walls were painted hospital green and it had that institutional feeling to it. My office was on the 3rd floor. When you entered my office, it was as if you left the building completely. I did everything possible to transform my office into a relaxing and up to date environment. My office was filled with beautiful plants. In one corner of the room I had an Areca Palm and in the window seal I had an African Violet and a Beach Spider Lily. On my desk was a Peace Lily. I love how plants transform a room and bring out its beauty. I considered my office my place of solitude. Yes, I had work to do but when I closed that office door this was my private place. I quickly reviewed my calendar for upcoming meetings and pulled out Amanda's file to review once more before heading out to visit the home. Amanda was 6 years old and in the first grade. She attended New Visions Elementary School. Half way through the school year and she has been absent from school 38 times. Teachers have reported bruises on her arms and legs. When they asked Amanda how she got the bruises, she said she fell. The mother was a stay at home mom and the stepfather worked at a Burlington Coat factory in Garden City, New York. They lived on Buffalo Avenue in Hempstead, NY. Amanda was a quiet student and her grades were average. I was visiting the home first and then I was going to stop by the school to see the child.

As I pulled up to the house I noticed two men sitting on the steps passing a liquor bottle between the two of them. The house needed a lot of repairs. It was a two-story house painted a dirty white with black trim. Shingles were hanging from the house; the small front lawn was not cared for and one of the windows was covered with a piece of wood. I understand that not everyone can afford the nicer things in life but it just seemed to me that a child should not have to grow up and live in a house like that. I sat in the car for a few minutes praying that the two men would leave. I did not want to have to walk pass them for fear of what they might say. I gathered my briefcase and I looked up and noticed one of the men left. He took the bottle of liquor with him. It was 10 am in the morning and too early to be drinking. As I approached the steps I noticed someone staring out of the upstairs window. I got to the steps and paused. "Is this the home of Mrs. Delores Glen? the man looked at me with a slight disdain, "who is asking?" "I am Mrs. Matthews and I am from Child Protective Services." He straightened up quickly and flashed a big smile at me. "I am Mr. Mitchell Glen and I can take you inside and get my wife." I followed him into the house and as I entered the house there was an old dank smell in the hallway. It was as if all the windows needed to be opened to air out the place. He showed me into the living room. The living room was a large room with old furniture. Most of the furnishings in the living room looked as if they were items picked up at a thrift store. On the small coffee table, there were empty plates with remnants of spaghetti dried up and starting to change color. Looks as if those plates may have been sitting there for a few days. On the end table, there were 3 empty beer cans. The sofa had old stains on it and was slightly lopsided. I chose to sit in the chair next to the sofa. Seconds after I sat down Dolores walks into the living room. "I not sure why someone would call CPS on us but we take good care of our child. She has a roof over her head and she has 3 meals a day". I politely interrupted her, "Mrs. Glen it is our job to investigate all complaints especially where there are visible injuries to a child. Now I am not saying that your daughter is not properly taken care of, I am just here to examine her living conditions and make a recommendation". Her husband grabbed her by the arm and said "Let's just let the lady do her job. We know we do our best so just cooperate." I started with the basic questions and received the basic answers. Then I asked about bruises on Amanda's legs and arms. Both confirmed that Amanda fell while playing outside. I noticed Mitchell rubbing his hands together in a nervous manner. The whole time I was taking notes of all responses and all that I observed. I then asked if I could see Amanda's bedroom. As they were leading me to the steps to go upstairs, I notice the condition of the kitchen. The sink was filled with dirty dishes and there were dirty dishes also on the kitchen table. The floor looked as if it had not mopped in months. In Amanda's room, there were piles of clothes in the corner on the floor. Her bed had no sheets on it, just a blanket. The mattress was stained and the dresser was missing the knobs to open the dresser. There were no pictures on the walls or any decorations that you would see in a little girl's room. The only toy I saw was a doll. What a gloomy existence for a child. I asked the parents how they discipline Amanda. "Well I am from the old school and I believe in spankings. My husband is usually the one who does the spanking but it is only when she really does something bad. Amanda is basically a good kid but she knows how to get on her father's nerves at times. You know when your man gets home from work he needs peace and quiet. Kids don't seem to get that and that usually gets her in trouble". There it is! She was protecting her husband and it seemed that it was more about her husband's needs rather than the needs of her child. Mr. Glen just stood there and allowed Delores to do all the talking. I had seen enough and really wanted to talk with the child. I was about to leave and I suddenly heard a whimpering sound coming from the bedroom down the hall. "Excuse me Mrs. Glen, is there someone else in the house?" "Oh yes, Amanda was not feeling well today and she stayed home from school today. When she is sick, I allow her to rest in my bedroom". "Can I please see Amanda?" She called for Amanda and she came down the hall wearing a dirty t-shirt and her underwear. I could clearly see the bruises on her legs and arms. And her face was tear stained. I just wanted to grab this little girl and run right out the door. "Hi Amanda, I am Mrs. Matthews and I would like to talk with you for a little bit. Come into your bedroom and we can talk. "Mr.

and Mrs. Glen, I would like to talk with Amanda alone for a few minutes if you don't mind." In a nervous voice, Delores gave her consent. "Now Amanda don't be afraid, I just want to get to know you." Surprisingly, Amanda was happy to talk and answer my questions. Amanda's mood quickly changed when I asked her about the bruises. "Amanda how did you get those bruises on your arms and legs?" Amanda took a few seconds before she answered. "I fell down the steps." That was all I needed to hear. Her story did not match Mom's story. I knew I was going to recommend that Amanda be removed from this home. The one thing that truly disturbed me was when Amanda said it hurt when she went to the bathroom. I wanted this child examined immediately. I told Mr. and Mrs. Glen that we would be in touch. I went to the office to file my report and my recommendation that the child be removed from the home. I hope that Amanda gets a chance at a normal life.

FOUR

CALVIN

After I finished writing my reports I called Crystal to confirm our dinner date. We had reservations at Pier 95 in Freeport. I loved this restaurant and my favorite dinner entre was their Oven Roasted Duck with wild blueberry sauce. And I needed a glass of wine. Crystal and I went to grade school together and we have remained friends since then. We tried to have dinner at least once a month. This was our time to catch up. Crystal was the only one who had a clue about my childhood. Not sure if she knew all the details but she did know that I had it hard. She never asked and I never told. I was forbidden to tell. But she was always there for me and a true friend. We met at 5pm for drinks and dinner was at 6pm. This was my time to unwind and be as close to the real me as possible. No pretenses, just me. We finished up around 8pm and I headed home.

I got home before David. I took a long hot shower and turned on the television. I watched the news and before I knew it I was asleep. I was not sure what time David got home but he did not wake me up. For that I was thankful. The next morning I went into work a little early because I needed to take a longer than usual lunch break. I left the office around 11am and headed to LaGuardia Airport. I parked in the short-term parking. I went to the JetBlue terminal and sat across from the customer check-in and there was Calvin checking in customer's luggage. I watched him with his wicked smile as he helped the customers. He looked just as slick as I always remembered him. I hated him just like I hated Felix. I sat there for 45 minutes just watching him and imagining him suffering and begging for his life. He was still a handsome man and I am sure he never had a shortage of women. I sat there and remembered the clammy feel of his hands when he would touch my skin. I remembered how he would whisper in my ear. Before I realized it, there were tears streaming down my cheek. An older woman sitting two seats away from me asked if I was ok. I said I was fine and I got up and left the airport. On the ride, back to my office, all I could think about was my plan. My plan was to make them all pay. The rest of the afternoon at work was uneventful and I spent most of the time finishing up paperwork. David called to see if I wanted to go out for dinner, but I just wanted to go home. I got home and took a hot shower and David ordered Chinese food for dinner. We watched Training Day starring Denzel Washington and I just laid in his arms. There were times that it felt like David understood me. He was not after me sexually every night. There were times he was ok with just holding me. He was so good to me and I wish I could be a better wife to him. I looked him in his eyes and said, "David, you do know that I love you with all of my heart?" He smiled ever so gently at me and said, "Of course I do and you do know that I love you with all of my heart and would do anything in this world to protect you?" I smiled, closed my eyes and cuddled in his arms. There were times I felt like I did not deserve him. I was so consumed with my past that I could not focus on becoming the wife he needed in the bedroom. Funny thing is, he never complained about our sex life and I never had a fear or reason to believe he was unfaithful. After the movie, we went to bed and instead of sex, he just held me until I fell asleep.

****

FIVE

PLAN IN MOTION

The next morning I waited until David left for work and I entered the details of my trip to the airport into my journal. I was working a half day today and then I was going to the Freeport Memorial Library. I had some research to do that required not using my laptop. I left work at noon and drove to the library. The library was established in 1884 and in 1982, during the Village of Freeport's 90th Anniversary the library was expanded. The landscaping around the building was beautiful and inside the library, I fell in love with stain glass high cathedral ceilings. With everything being online today, it is a wonder that libraries can keep their doors open. I love being in the library and physically holding a book in my hands. But today it was not about reading a book. I needed to use their computers to do some research. I found an empty computer that was away from the cluster of computers and sitting in a corner. I sat down and turn on the computer. I logged into the computer as a guest user and pulled up Google search engine. I searched for poisons that can't be traced. Potassium chloride. One of our friends who happens to be a doctor, once said, "they do not detect any poisons that they do not test for and they rarely test for poisons. But I needed to be sure. I came across one that was interesting. Botulinum toxin, very powerful nerve agent. In small quantities, it is used in anti-aging treatments. and the familiar term is Botox. Botulism is the term for Botox poisoning. In injection form, it can be lethal. The vengeful side wanted to see this through to the end.

No one knows the endless pain that I have suffered and continue to suffer. Thoughts of revenge have consumed me and robbed me of my happiness. I used to attend church faithfully but I knew I had to leave the church. I had to leave because I knew if I developed a relationship with God then I would not be able to go through with my plans. I needed this so bad regardless of what I lost in the end. I wrapped up my research and headed home, but I made a detour. I needed to see Larry first.

SIX

LARRY

I hated Larry the most. I hated him more than Felix or Calvin. He was a construction site manager and his crew was working on a project on North Ocean avenue. They were working on constructing a bank at that location. I parked across the street and scanned the area until I spotted him. As I watched him, I could imagine cutting his throat and watching him beg with his eyes for mercy. Larry was the devil and I hated him for how he has stolen a piece of me. I started my car and drove slowly past the work site but he never looked my way. I drove home feeling emotionally drained. I took a shower and cooked dinner for my husband. He was so surprised and he showed his appreciation by making love to me. But for the first time I could not fake it. My mind would not leave the thoughts of Larry. David looked at me with a curious look and said, "where were you?" "I am not feeling too well. I am sorry." David was no dummy. "No that was different. You were disconnected. Do you want to talk? I am always here for you if you need to talk." Oh, how I wish I could talk to David but I feared he would not understand or worst yet he would not respect or love me any longer. I just smiled at him and said, "I love you and I don't need to talk about anything, I am just not feeling good. I laid in the bed until I heard his gentle snoring. I turned on my side and cried myself to sleep. As I went through the rest of my week I often thought about Felix, Calvin and Larry. I hated that the they occupied space in my thoughts. It seemed so unfair that they be allowed the luxury of my thoughts, but I was obsessed and I could not control my thoughts when it came to those three.

****

SEVEN

DETOUR

I woke up Saturday morning and my stomach was so upset and I threw up twice. I took a shower and went and laid back down. David stuck his head in the bedroom door, "Wow I don't think I have ever seen you get back in the bed after getting up. Are you ok?" "I am not feeling to well this morning. Stomach virus or even maybe food poisoning. I just need to rest a little longer." He came over and felt my forehead, "well you don't have a fever and you seem cool. I am going to the gym but I will stop back home after to check on you." He planted a kiss on my forehead and left. At 11 am I got up and started my day. Sunday morning, the same thing happened again, stomach ache and vomiting. All week the same thing but I started to get up before David and pull myself together because I did not want him worrying about me. I was having lunch with Crystal and she said to me, "Could you be pregnant?" "Hell no. Plus, I am on birth control and I take my pill every day." Crystal's questions stayed with me all day, "Could you be pregnant?" I called my doctor to see what was the earliest I could see her. I was lucky because she had an afternoon cancellation. I got to Dr. Wilson's office at 3 pm and did not have long to wait. I was asked for a urine sample when I went to the bathroom. I waited for the doctor to review my test results and she finally came into the room. "Roxanne how are you doing?" "I am fine just getting sick daily." She looked at me and said, "I assume by daily you mean in the morning? Well that is because you are pregnant." Of course, she is smiling and so happy for me while I am sitting here in a state of shock. "Dr. Wilson, how is that possible? I have been taking my pill daily." "Is it possible you might have skipped a day without realizing it?" I just could not believe this was happening. There was no way I could have this baby. "Dr. Wilson, I can't have this baby. I need to have an abortion and I need you to be discreet about it. My husband must not know that I am pregnant." Dr. Wilson had a surprised look on her face. "I am your doctor and I am legally bound from telling anyone your medical condition. Are your sure this is what you want? Do you think you should take a few days and think about it?" "There is no way I can have this baby and I do not want to think about it. Can you recommend someone to do the procedure?" She was hesitant but she provided me the name and address of a doctor who specialized in abortions. I also asked her was there anything she could give me to the help with morning sickness? Unfortunately, there were no medications she could give me. As soon as I got in my car I called the abortion clinic. They had availability for the procedure on Wednesday. That gave me two days to make plans that would not lead David to become suspicious.

That evening when I got home, I told David that I needed to go out of town for a last-minute week long business training. "One of my co-workers was scheduled to attend but had a family emergency at the last minute. The training is in Boston and I need to fly out first thing in the morning." He looked disappointed but assured me that he understood. "I will drop you off at the airport in the morning." I told David that I wrote a list for some things I needed from the store. "No problem. I will go to the store now and I am going to stop by dad's house really quick to check on him." David's dad lived alone and he would check on his dad regularly because of his age and heath conditions. As soon as David left and I was sure he had driven off, I picked up the phone and dialed Crystal's number. The phone rang 5 times and Crystal finally picked up. "Girl I really need your help!" She was curious. "What's up?" "I need to crash at your place for about 1 week. Please don't ask any questions now because I will explain every-thing tomorrow when I see you. I will need you to pick me up from the airport tomorrow around 8 am." I could image the look on Crystal's face and the inquisitiveness dancing on her face. I know she was dying to know what was going on, but Crystal did not ask or pry. "I will be there and yes we must talk." "Love you girl and see you in the morning." I could not think beyond the week that I was supposed to be gone for training but problem was it took longer than a week to heal from an abortion. And how do I avoid sex with David until I am healed. I think I will need to get sick when I get back from train-ing. I will work those minor details out when I return. I really hated lying to David but I was doing this to protect our marriage. I didn't think our relationship was ready for a child but most importantly I don't think I was mentally equipped to be a mother. I needed to deal with the issues in my life before thinking about bringing a life into this world. When David re-turned, I finished packing and of course he felt the need to make love to me before I left. I did not fight it since I would not see him for a week. The next day David got me to the airport by 7 am and Crystal was not picking me up until 8 am so I went and purchased a newspaper and sat there and read the newspaper. Crystal was right on time and we rode to her apartment in silence. When we were finally relaxing she just look at me and said, "what is going on girl? Are you and David having problems?" I smiled and reassured her that David and I were fine. "Crystal, I am pregnant." Crystal jumped up. "Wow that is wonderful. But from the look on you face, I am not so sure that it is wonderful news." I wasn't exactly smiling and bursting with joy. "No, it is not wonderful news and the reason I asked to stay with you is I plan on having an abortion. Things are going well between David and I but I am not ready to have a child." Crystal had a puzzled look on her face. "I am confused. You say that things are great, then what is wrong with having a baby and if you decided on an abortion doesn't David have the opportunity to voice he opinion since this is his child also?" There was a part of me that felt I should tell her everything but I was not sure I was ready for a sharing session. "Crystal I really need you to trust me. There is so much I need to tell you but I am not ready and it has nothing to do with you but for you to understand I would need to tell it all and that would be like reliving some things I am not ready to relive. I am just asking for trust and loyalty. I will explain it all when I am ready." God truly blessed me with a special person as it pertains to Crystal because she was everything you could ask for in a friend. She did not push and was willing to wait until I was ready to talk. Crystal took time off work to make sure she was with me during the abortion. I called David to let him know that I arrived safely in Boston. I prepared for the abortion but there was a little nervousness in me. There was life inside of me growing and I was about to extinguish it without hesitation.

I was up early Wednesday morning in the bathroom sick to my stomach. It was a combination of morning sickness and nervous sickness. I took a shower and got dress. Crystal and I did not talk much as we got ready to go to the clinic. When we got in the car, Crystal looked at me and gently took my hand, "are you sure this is what you want to do? Whatever you decide to do, I will be there for you." For the first time since I arrived at Crystal's apartment I cried. It was that release that I needed. "Crystal I love you and I could not ask for a better friend, but this is something I have to do. No I am not happy about it but once it is over I promise I will talk to you and hopefully shed some light on my decision. Right now, I just need to go and get this over with. We arrived at the clinic at 8:30am and there were four other women in the waiting area. Only one of the women was with a man. I sat there and wondered what was their stories and why were they here? Did we share the same reasons for taking life? I sat there for 20 minute before they called my name. Crystal stood up to go with me and I stopped her, "I need to do this by myself." She hugged me and I went with the nurse. I undressed and put on a hospital gown. Everything from that point on was a blur until I woke up in the recovery room. I was cramping bad and still groggy from the anesthesia. I just wanted to sleep but the nurse insisted that I wake up. See gave me something for the pain. Forty-five minutes later I was walking out the door. Crystal and I rode in silence as I drifted in and out of sleep. It was 1:30pm when we got to Crystal's apartment and all I wanted to do was sleep. When I finally woke up, it was 9:30pm. I called David and we talked for about ten minutes and I said I was so tired from all day training and meetings and just wanted to get some sleep. I said goodnight.

EIGHT

CONFESSION

Crystal came into the guest room where I was staying. "Are you hungry? I did not want to wake you." I was not hungry but I thought it was finally time that Crystal and I talked. I have never shared any of my past with anyone and I was glad to be able to share with someone finally. "Well it started with Felix. After my father died from a drug overdose, my mother started bringing different men into our home. She never stayed with any of them more than a couple of weeks until she met Felix. She fell hard for Felix. She worked overtime to please Felix. I was about ten years old when he moved into our home. Shortly after that they

got married. Everyone but my mother knew that
Felix had a wondering eye and loved the ladies.
When Felix did not come home, I would hear
my mother in her bedroom crying. When he
came home she would start arguing with him
but he would tell her that he loved her and no
one else and the argument was over. Felix was
always very nice to me and always told me that I
was a pretty-little girl. He always commented
on what I was wearing. He made a habit of asking for a kiss and always insisted that I call him
daddy. I never found comfort in calling him
daddy. I came home from school one afternoon
and mom was not home but Felix was home and
he was drinking. He asked me about school and
then said come and give your daddy a hug. This
hug made me feel very uncomfortable. He held
me longer than usual and his hands slipped
down around my waist and he pulled me tight
to his body. This did not feel right and I wanted
to be free of his embrace. When he released me,
I went into my bedroom. I was scared and I
stayed there until my mother got home. From

that day on I tried to make sure I was not alone with Felix. That did not save me. I was asleep one night and Felix came into my room and slipped into my bed. I was scared to move. I asked him why was he in my bed. He said when I was sleep I called out in my sleep and he thought I was having a bad dream. He was just comforting me. I did not like it and I called out for my mother and he said my mother was not home. He told me I did not need to tell her about this because she would over react and would not believe me. That night he raped me and that was the first of many nights I had to endure. I tried to tell my mother but she shut me down quickly. As she put it, I must have misunderstood and I needed to stop leading him on. At ten years old how could I possibly be leading this grown man on. My mother made her choice that night and it was not me. I tried to avoid him as much as possible but at night it was difficult to avoid him. When I saw him drinking, I knew I would get a visit in my bedroom that night. I often wonder how could my mother not know and she was willing to sacrifice her daughter for the sake of keeping a man that was not worth keeping. I endured this for months and I had no one to confide in and no one to turn to for help. I was forced to see and experience the ugliness that existed in this world. At ten years old I should have been shielded and protected from the ugliness. I thought that this was the worst that any child would have to endure. Until Calvin came along. Calvin was my mother's brother and he was a functioning drunk. Felix and Calvin got along very well because they were two of a kind. Both were womanizers, drunks and pedophiles. One night Calvin came over for a poker game. There were four other men there that I did not know. They played poker, drank liquor and smoked marijuana. My mother waited on them like a maid. She was the only woman there while they were playing cards. It was approximately two in the morning when I started hearing the men leave. The only men that were left were Felix and Calvin. They were still drinking and Felix told my mother to leave them alone and go to bed. She did exactly as she was told. I decided to stop eavesdropping and finally go to bed. Just as I was about to go to sleep my bedroom door opened and I peeped from under my cover and saw both Felix and Calvin standing in my bedroom. I became so scared because deep down I knew what was about to happen. I tried to pretend I was sleep as I heard Felix say, "I told you that she was a young sweet thing." That one sentenced confirmed what was about to happen. They took turns taking advantage of me and that night I cried all night long. That following morning I wanted to end my life. I did not think I could go through life knowing that my stepfather and my uncle raped me. I took a bottle of pills from the medicine cabinet and laid down in my bed and closed my eyes. I am not sure who found me or how I ended up in the hospital. But when I came to I was in a lot of pain. There was a woman sitting by my bedside. She looked at me, "wow nice to see you awake. My name is Mrs. Douglas and I am a counselor and I just wanted to talk with you for a few minutes." I already knew why she was here but could she possibly be my savior in disguise. Could she take me out of my home? Or better yet, should I tell her what has happened to me. As quickly as those thoughts came they left me when I thought about the possibility of Felix hurting me or my mom.

In time the rapes were less frequent. Years of being raped by my stepfather and my uncle. The darkest days of my life or so I thought." Crystal sat there speechless as I share my nightmare with her. She grabbed my hand and held on tightly. "I knew you had it rough but I had no idea. I wish I would have known." I looked at her with a loving smile, "there was nothing you could have done." She let my hand go and got up. "I am going to make you something to eat. You must eat and personally I can't hear any more of this right now. My heart hurts for you because this secret has stood in the way of your true happiness. You did not deserve to be hurt this way as a child and I am glad it did not leave you vengeful and bitter." I looked her straight in the eye, "Oh but you are so wrong." That statement left her speechless. "Roxanne, you have to find a way to let this go. Have you thought about seeing someone?" I knew she meant well. "A shrink? no I have not given any thought to seeing a shrink. Besides I don't want some stranger trying to get inside of my head. I will be fine. I just need you to swear that you will never repeat what I have told you, no matter what. I am ok and I will have bad days and good days but I have made it thus far." She looked at me with such pity. She squeezed my hand and promised to keep my secret and never tell. I ate a little and went back to sleep. I was tired and not quite so ready to tell her about Larry. I hated Larry the most. I was always told that hate is a strong word but that was the best word to describe what I was feeling. At that moment, I just wanted the peace of sleeping and not thinking.

****

NINE

I FAILED AMANDA

Crystal took excellent care of me the whole week. It was time for me to get myself together and go home to David. I called David to let him know what time I would be getting to the airport. Crystal dropped me off at the airport an hour before David was supposed to pick me up. I really did not like lying to David, but this was to protect him in the long run. As I was walking through the airport I saw Calvin. It was too late for me to turn the other way because he saw me. "Roxanne? Is that you?" I froze and I could not find my voice at first. Then I began to walk away, "Yes, it is me but I don't have time to chat. I am in hurry." I quickly moved on as he stood there looking at me as if he was in shock. My heart start racing and I could not catch my breath. When I was out of his eye sight, I stopped to catch my breath and calm down. I hated that I felt so out of control in the presence of that monster. I did not want him to ever have any type of control over me. I saw David's car outside of the revolving doors. I was happy to see David and ready to go home. When I got in the car, I did not get the greeting I was expecting. David gave me a hug and kiss but he had sadness written all over his face. First, I thought something was wrong with his father but what he told me was like slicing a vein open. "Baby I am sorry to have to tell you this but Amanda was murdered." I could not and did not want to believe what I had heard. I instantly collapsed into tears. As I cried, all I could think about was I failed this little girl. Once I could pull myself together I asked David what happened? "The news report stated that preliminary report say that she was beaten severely and during the beating she fell and hit her head on the corner of the end table in her living room. They have arrested her mother and step-father." I could not believe what I was hearing. "I thought they were removing the child from the home?" David said according to the news article there were delays with the paperwork so the child was not immediately removed. All I could think about at that moment was, I failed her. I believe David saw it in my face. "You can't start blaming yourself. No one could have known that this would happen and you did the best you could do under the circumstances." I felt the anger building inside me. The rage was growing and I thought about Felix, Calvin and Larry. If we could only rid the world of monsters like this. When we got home, I told David that I was exhausted and I want to go to bed. There was no argument there. Before I went to sleep, I pulled out my journal and wrote about what happened over the last week. The following morning I was up early. I prepared breakfast and left the house before David was awake. I left him note and left it under his coffee cup. I was about to do something that could cost me my job but I had to do it. I was going to Riker's Island to see Delores Glen. I needed to see her. I knew this was against all the rules but I needed to know how she could allow this to happen. What was she thinking? Did love of a man cause you to turn your back on your daughter? I needed answers. It was a 40 minute drive to Riker's island if I took the Southern State parkway and Grand Central parkway. After I arrived and got on the bus to the Island I started thinking, what was I doing? I thought about turning around and going home but it was only a thought. When I finally came face to face with Delores she looked like a broken and defeated person. As she walked towards me, she had a blank stare on her face. She sat down and said nothing. "Delores, do you remember me?" She looked up at me and then lowered her head. It was as if she was lowering her head in shame. "I remember you. You came to my house to investigate why there were bruises on my child." I looked at this shell of a woman and wanted to feel pity for her but I couldn't. Only thing I could feel was scorn and disdain. How could you not do everything in your power to protect your child? I would kill to protect my child. As soon as that thought entered my mind, I thought about the child that I just killed. As I looked at her, she could not look me in my eyes. "Delores, can you just tell me why?" She lifted her head and stared into my eyes. "Don't judge me!! You could never understand what I went through trying to be a loving wife. It was not easy having a daughter around that took the attentions of my husband. I began to despise her. She is the reason I am here rotting away instead of with my husband." I sat there in disbelief. I could not believe what just came out of her mouth. I realized at that point that this woman was sick. Nothing I could say would help this situation. My heart was breaking for Amanda and I had no room for pity for this monster sitting in front of me. In my eyes, she was just as guilty as her husband. I stood up to leave and looked her in the eyes; "May your remaining

days be filled with torment." I could not understand such evil.

TEN

THE TIME IS NOW

When I got in my car, I closed my eyes and asked God for forgiveness. I know that I was wrong for wishing torment on that woman. Actually, it was kind of ironic that I was asking for forgiveness knowing what I was planning. My phone starting ringing and it was David. I really did not want to talk with David right now. I just let the call go to voicemail. I sat in my car for an hour. I cried and they were tears of anger. I was so filled with emotion that I just sat there until I became calm. My drive home was as if I had an out of body experience. I went home and went to sleep. I was awoken to David sitting on the bed next to me. "Hey Sunshine, are you feeling ok?" This was my opportunity to claim sickness to avoid intimacy so I could continue to heal. "Actually, I am not feeling too good. I think I might have picked up a bug. I came home and had to lie down because I felt horrible." He was so understanding and proceeded to taking care of his sick wife. He came back into the bedroom with a curious look on his face. "Hey just wondering where you went so early this morning. I woke up and you were gone." I didn't expect that question. "I went into work early because I woke up feeling crappy so I decided to go in and get a few things done and come home. Sorry but I didn't want to wake you." He looked satisfied with my answer. I spent the day laying around the house and writing in my journal. I decided that it was time to execute my plan for Felix. My phone rang and I did not recognize the phone number. I hesitated but finally answered the phone. "Was there something I could help you with?" My heart dropped and it felt like I stopped breathing. I could not find my voice.

"What's wrong, the cats got your tongue? Listen up; I am not sure why you are lurking around my job but you need to back off. Unless you are missing me and need something special from me." The words were stuck in my mouth. I couldn't say anything. I just hung up the phone. I sat there trembling. How did he get my phone number? I sat on the edge of my bed terrified and memories just bombarded me. I could imagine his touch, his smell, his breath and his threats. I was so overwhelmed with these memories until I became light-headed. The room started spinning and I just lied down and cried myself to sleep. The following day I was up early and David awoke while I was drying off from my shower. "Hey where do you think you are going? Are you feeling up to going to work today?" I assured him I was still not feeling myself. "I am going into work to fill out some paper work. I need to be honest with you David. I need some time away from work because Amanda's death took a toll on me. I am going to take a leave of absence just to get my head straight and focus on some personal projects. I hope I have your support on this." He got out of the bed, came over and held me. "I did not realize just how Amanda's death would affect you. I support you 100% and you take as much time as you need. Do you want me to drive you to work?" All I could think was, you are too good for me. "No I will be just fine. I still feel crappy but a little better than yesterday. I won't be gone long and I will call you at work once I get back home." I finished getting dressed and left before David did.

When I got to work, my boss wanted to speak with me. She basically gave me a speech about not blaming myself for what happened to Amanda. I told her that I needed to take a leave of absence and she gave me her approval. I took a six-month leave of absence with the option to return sooner if I was ready. I had one more stop before going home. I was going to meet with Carlos. Carlos was a very shady character that I grew up with and went to school with. While most of us grew up and got respectable jobs, Carlos became a low life drug peddler. I always spoke to Carlos when I saw him and never treated him differently. I think that is one reason he would do anything for me. Others avoided him like he was the plague. I am no one's judge and as I learned in church, we are all sinners saved by grace. In Carlos and my case I don't think we got to the saved part. There was not a drug around that Carlos could not get his hands on. Not sure how and who his connections were and I did not want to know. I contacted Carlos last week and told him that I need a vial of Botulinum toxin. He did not ask any questions and said give him a couple of days to get the drug. As much as Carlos liked me, there was still a cost involved. He gave me his family discount, so it cost me $500. I met him at Glacken Park and we transacted our business. As I drove home, I began to think and question my sanity. Who does this? But I was driven by the hurt and the pain. I knew what needed to be done for me to be released and freed. When I got home I sat down and started to put my plan into play. I decided I would visit Felix first. In two days, I would drop by the nursing home to see Felix. I prayed that he would have one vivid memory of me being with him on that day. I got home and started writing in my journal. As I was writing I thought about that phone call. How did Larry get my phone number and I was so sure he did not see me that day I went to his job? I was still shaken up by that phone call and I thought Larry would be the hardest. I had to think through my plan for Larry very carefully. The next two days I just laid around the house and let David wait on me hand and foot. The night before I was going to visit Felix, David asked me something that caught me totally off guard. "Do you think you should see a psychiatrist? It might be helpful with all of the stress you have been under lately." I was not sure what he meant by all the stress because only thing that was really stressful was hearing about the death of Amanda and anyone who was personally involved would feel some stress. What was he trying to insinuate? "Why would you think that I need to see a shrink?" He quickly changed his tone, "No don't misunderstand, I just thought you might want to talk to someone who specializes in death of a child. I just want the best for you and make sure you are comfortable". I let it go as quick as he asked the question. I reassured him that I did not need a psychiatrist. I just needed some time off work and I would be fine. There was something different about David but I could not put my finger on it. I could not let that distract me because tomorrow I was going to visit Felix.

ELEVEN

GOODBYE FELIX

The next morning I was up bright and early. David was still sleep and I went in the kitchen and called Crystal. "Hey girl, if David asks, please say I was with you today." There was silence on the phone line. "I am not sure I want to be a part of your lies to David. I am not sure what is going on with you Roxanne but I am scared for you. You can't keep lying to David." Wow my girl was changing right before my eyes. I had to be careful how I answered her because right now she was the only ally that I had. "Listen Crystal I have decided to see a shrink to help me deal with my issues and I am not ready for David to know. In time, I

will talk to him but I have to work on me first."
"Oh, Roxanne I am so happy you have finally
decided to get help and yes I will make sure I
don't tell David. Anything I can do please just let
me know. And Roxanne I love you and want the
best for you. I am proud of this first step that
you are taking." Hated lying to Crystal but I
needed her in my camp. "I love you too and
thanks for always being in my corner." After I
finished my call to Crystal, I prepared breakfast
for David. "I see you are up early and dressed.
What are your plans for today?" David had a
different look in his eyes. "I am going to spend
the day with Crystal. I just need to get of the
house today." He came over and embraced me
and planted a gentle kiss on my lips. Something
was so different about David. "I want you to
know that I love you more that you will ever
know. You mean the world to me." I did not
have time to deal with David right now. "I love
you too. What's up with you? Sounding like
you are about to leave for an extended period."
He smiled, "I just felt I needed to let you know

that I love you. And no there is nothing wrong just thinking about how lucky I am." After David left for work, it was time to leave for the nursing home. As I drove all I could think about was, "would he know me?"

After I parked my car, I walked into the nursing home full of anxiety. I stop at the reception desk. "I am here to see my stepfather, Felix Rodriguez." The nurse was very pleasant. She smiled at me and asked me to sign in. As I walked down the hall towards Felix's room, all I could think about was the vial that was in my coat pocket. My heart was racing but it was not panic as much as it was a feeling of pending victory. I entered his room and there he was slumped in the chair near the window. His eyes had that blank gaze and I quickly look away. There were some things I needed to say first. "Felix I honestly hope that you understand and know who I am because it is important that you know just how much pain you have caused me. A child should have memories of the innocence in their life. As an adult, you should be able to think about your past with joy and not be concerned with the harsh realities of life. I tried to avoid memories of my childhood. Memories of a dark room and a monster running his hands between my thighs, a monster penetrating my private and forcing himself upon me. I have a lifetime of nightmares and it is difficult for me to be intimate with any man. My life has been stolen from me because of you and other monsters like you. Many might say that I should try to forget but you consume and take up so much space in my mind. I am not sure that ridding the world of you will silence the memories but I know no other way. Because of you I question my sanity on a regular basis. I have cried so much until I have run out of tears. And worst of all I took life. I denied my husband the opportunity of having a child. I am not sure you will ever understand just what you have done to me. I want you to suffer and I want the last face that you see to be mine." I walked over to where he was seated. I pulled the syringe from my pocket and when I put my hand on his shoulder, he just slumped over. Slumped over dead!! I just sat on the edge of the bed and began to cry. I was not crying because Felix was dead, I was crying because I was not the reason for his death. I was robbed of the opportunity to exact my vengeance. Then I noticed something from the side of his hospital gown. Was it blood? Was he bleeding? I was not sure where the blood was coming from. I grabbed the call button and pushed it. The nurses aide stuck her head in the door. "How can I help you?" "Mr. Rodriguez is bleeding and unresponsive," As I stood there, doctors and nurses started rushing into the room. I was asked to leave. I sat in the lobby in a daze until I heard the police siren. I got up to leave and one of the nurses stop me, "Mrs. please don't leave because the police might want to speak with you." I looked at her with a curious expression. "Why are the police here and why would they want to talk with me?" As the police officer was walking in my direction, the nurse said, "Mr. Rodriguez was stabbed." I could not believe what I was hearing. "Mrs. Matthews, can I speak with privately for a moment." I looked at the police officer and I complied. We went into the employee break room. "Mrs. Matthews, can you tell me what happened when you went in to see Mr. Rodriguez?" I sat down and began to tell the police officer what happened. "When I went in to see Felix, he was sitting in a chair near the window. I began talking to him but I did not notice anything until I got closer and saw the blood. I first touched his shoulder and he slumped over and that is when I noticed the blood. I then called for assistance." He was taking notes and then he looked up. "What is your relationship with Mr. Rodriguez?" "He was my stepfather." The next question put me on guard. "What was the relationship like between you and Mr. Rodriguez?" Where was this conversation headed? "Should I contact a lawyer?" "Why do you think that you would need a lawyer?" I did not like the line of questioning. "Our relationship was fine and he was like that before I entered his room." I guess the police officer sensed my irritation. "Mrs. Matthews, these are routine questions we have to ask and we have determined that he was stabbed before you arrived." I put my hands in my coat pocket and came across the vial. I needed to be calm and not give them no reason to notice my nervousness. "Mrs. Matthews, that is all and we will contact you if we have any other questions." I began to walk out of the room and turned back. "Any ideas who killed him?" The officer stood up, "This is an open investigation and you know I can't discuss it with you. Have a good day." I left the building and I welcomed the fresh air. I walked to the car and I was literally in a daze. Someone beat me to Felix. Someone stole the opportunity for vengeance from me. Instead of feeling sad for Felix, I was angry that someone got to him first. I needed him to know what he did to me and how much pain he caused me. But who? Was there some other woman that he took advantage of and she was seeking revenge? My mind was racing trying to come up with a logical explanation to what just happened. I needed to come up with some believable story for David because he would hear about this and know that I was here. That would be easy because David was not aware of my feelings towards Felix. As far as David was concern my relationship with my stepfather was fine. I got home before David and took a nice hot shower. I was lying on the couch in the living room when David got home. He came rushing in the house. "Hey baby, did you hear about Felix?" I sat up and tried to look heartbroken. "I was the one who found him. I decided to stop by to see how he was doing before going to Crystal's apartment. Who would do such a thing to a man in a nursing home?" David held me in his arms and tried to comfort me. "I was supposed to go and sit with my father tonight but I will cancel because you need me more right now." I needed to be alone right now. "I will not hear of that, you go and be with your father. He needs you and I will be fine." He was hesitant but I convinced him to go. Shortly after David left, my phone rang. It was my mother and I did not want to talk to her. I just let it ring. A few minutes later I got a text message. My mother was a persistent woman. She wanted to see me as soon as possible to talk about Felix. I knew she was not expecting any sympathy from me. For the sake of entertainment, I agreed to see her. I told her to stop by the house in a few minutes. She must have been around the corner because in less than five minutes she was ringing the doorbell. I opened the door. "Well that was quick. Come in and I am not in the mood for arguing tonight. What do you want?" She went to sit down. "Did you hear what happened to Felix today?" "Yes, I did. I was the one who discovered him." She look at me with accusatory eyes. "Why did you go to see him?" I turned on her quickly. "You have no right to question me and I do not think I owe you any explanation and I am not obligated to tell you anything. Now if you don't mind I am tired and ready to go to bed." She stood up to leave but turned around and said "If you are in trouble, I can help you." Now I was becoming furious. "I am not sure why you think I need anything from you. All I need from you right now is to leave my house." She left but not before saying, "I love you and I am sorry for not protecting you." I could not believe she had the nerve to say that. "A little late for sorry and I would prefer that you leave me alone. And for the record, I am glad he is dead and I am just sorry I could not have been the one to put him out of his misery." I slammed the door shut. There will come the day that I confront my mother but today was not that day. My phone began to ring again. It was Crystal and I guess the news about Felix was spreading. I really did not feel like talking to her but I needed to keep her in my corner, so I answered the phone. "Hey Crystal I guess you heard about Felix?" I figured I would get straight to the point. "Yes it was all over the news. I just wanted to make sure you were ok." "I am fine. I was the one who found him. I stopped over to the nursing home to talk to him about how he has made me feel. My shrink suggested that would be good healing for me to confront him. Well that never happen because when I got there he was already dead." Lying was becoming real easy for me. "Wow that had to be hard on you. I am so glad you are working on getting past your pain and moving on with your life. Well anytime you need someone to talk to, you know you can count on me." That was so true because she was the one person I could depend on. "I know that and I love you. I am exhausted and I just want to get some sleep, so I will talk to you later."

The next few days I was really thinking about Felix and should I abandon my plans. After seeing Felix lifeless body, I started thinking, who gave me the right to take a life? I hated that I was feeling this way because no one felt sorry or had second thoughts about the pain and suffering that I endured. I started going to the gym and it was amazing how a good workout rejuvenated you and I felt like I could take on the world. It also, somehow kept me focused.

TWELVE

****

GET IN LINE CALVIN

It was Calvin that I had to focus on now. I had to think how I was going to make him pay. He was not like Felix. He was in his right mind so he would understand what was going to happen to him. Carlos got me a drug that paralyzes you but you are awake and conscious of everything that is happening to you. I just had to figure out when I could get him alone and get close enough to him to inject him. The only option I could think about was going to his house. I knew where Calvin lived but I had never been to his house. Between Felix, Calvin and Larry, Calvin was the weakest and more of the follower. In my eyes that made no

difference because he knew right from wrong. I
didn't have Calvin's phone number and I did not
want to ask my mother because I felt like she
was already suspicious. My only option was to
go to the airport and talk to him. I decided I
would stop by the airport the following day to
arrange a meeting at his house. Under what pre-
tense I was not quite sure but I would come up
with something believable. I went into the bedroom to write in my journal before David got
home.   The following morning I waited until
David left for work and I drove to the airport.
As I parked my car and began to walk into the
JetBlue terminal, my heart was racing. I had not
spoken to Calvin in years and I was not sure
how he would react. There he was at the counter checking people in and taking their luggage.
Looking at him from a distance was one thing
but up close was something else entirely. I felt
like I was standing there for an eternity watching him. Time stood still and I was frozen. I
was realizing just how scared I was and I felt like
I could not go through with it. I finally walk

over to his counter and he looked up at me as though he had seen a ghost. "Hi Calvin. I was wondering if we could talk. I was wondering if I could stop by your place tomorrow." He looked totally speechless. "What is this all about?" "I just need to talk to you and I would prefer to discuss this in private." "Well I guess you can stop by around noon because tomorrow is my day off." "Thank you and see you then." When that was over, I was sweating and my heart was racing. I missed the opportunity with Felix but I was not going to miss Calvin or Larry. They both are going to pay and most of all they will know the pain and suffering I went through. Something told me that Larry would not care because he was evil incarnated. That night when David got home, he was super attentive. He suggested that under the circumstances we should spend the day together. He said he would take the day off from work. I insisted that I was ok. "How about you go to work because I have errands to run and we regroup after work for quality time together. A movie and dinner sounds great, right?" He agreed after some persuasion.

The following morning I was up before David, only because I was nervous about my meeting with Calvin. I prepared breakfast for David and that took him by surprise. "Hey baby this is a nice surprise. You feeling better?" I guess it was time to make myself available to David again. "Yes, I am feeling a lot better physically. Mentally, I am not ready to return to work. So, while I am home, I will do some spoiling my husband." He came up behind me and put his arms around my waist and kissed my neck. "You mean the world to me and I love you. You take all the time you need." I was so lucky to have a husband like David. "Hey I have a question to ask you." Oh boy, this sounded serious. "Sure, what is it?" He took both my hands into his. "Let's go to church on Sunday." Wow this really caught me off guard. It has been years since we had been to church. What was this all about? With what I was planning today, church was farthest from mind. Was God trying to tell me something? "Wow, definitely a change of pace. What brought this on?" "I just thought it would be nice. And time for us to re-focus and try a little Jesus in our life." "Well since you put it that way, how could I say no? Church on Sunday it is." When he left for work, I was left with some conflicted feelings. There was a sense of right and wrong that was embedded in me but I needed to do this. I did not need this doubt creeping up now of all times. What was done to me was not right and they should pay. I needed to shake this and get ready. And why suddenly did David have the desire to go to church? I did not need this right now. I needed to stay focus on the task at hand. It was time for me to get dressed and head to Calvin's place. As I was getting dressed, I began thinking about my past and remembered my mother telling me I was forbidden to tell anyone the stories I made up. She rather believe that I was making up these stories than believe her man could be molesting her daughter. That is the kind of love I could not comprehend. I left the house headed to Calvin's and a calm came over me. I was prepared to carry out my mission. When I arrived at Calvin's house, I sat in the car for a few moments. I removed the syringe from my purse and put it in my coat pocket. When I got to the front door, I went to ring the door bell and noticed the door was ajar. Could he have left the door open for me? Unlikely, but I entered and called out his name. No answer and I started to get the feeling that something was wrong. I called out his name again and as I walked toward the living room, I could see two legs on the floor stretched out. As I got closer, I could see that there was a body lying on the floor. It was Calvin's lifeless body lying there motionless on the floor. My head starting spinning. What was going on? First Felix and now Calvin. I was extremely careful not to touch anything. I made a u turn, took out a handkerchief from my purse and wiped the doorknob that I touch. I left the door ajar and as I left the house I looked around to see if there was anyone that I could see that would notice me leaving the house. No one in sight. I quickly got in my car and drove off. Was he dead? I did not want to hang around to find out. This was so unreal. Was it murder like Felix or an accident. This was all just crazy. I wondered if Larry was still amongst the living? I went home and started to call Crystal but hesitated. I felt like I needed someone to talk to but I had to be careful and not get careless. I was being cheated out of my justice. I guess in a sense they were getting what they deserved. But I was not the deliverer of justice and it did not sit well with me.

Late that evening my phone started ringing and it was my mother. I really did not want to speak with her because I was trying to wrap my head around what just happened. The phone stopped ringing and 5 seconds later it started ringing again. Wow she really was being persistent. "Hey. I am not in the mood to talk this evening. What do you want?" She let out a long sigh. "Well I really don't care about your mood. I need to talk to you and I mean now.

Not sure what you are up to but you are not right!" Ok enough of being nice. "What the hell are you talking about?" "I am on my way over and you better open the door." I was not sure what her problem was but she really did not want to go to war with me tonight. I was glad that David decided to go spend some time with his father tonight so I did not have to pretend to be nice. Twenty minutes later my doorbell rang. When I opened the door, my mother just brushed right past me. She looked as if she had been crying. "Are you behind any of this? I know you hated them!!" Now it started to make sense. She thought I was somehow involved with the deaths of Felix and Calvin. She did not know that I had been to Calvin's house because that would have fueled her suspicions. "The nerve of you to come over her and accuse me of anything. I wish I was the one who put both of those pigs out of their misery, but I was not fortunate enough to get that opportunity." She sat down as if she was defeated. "I know that you will never forgive me for what I did or ever understand but there comes a point in your life that you have to let the past go. Part of letting go is forgiving. Forgiveness sets you free. I am only telling you this because I had to learn to forgive to move on and part of that was forgiving myself. I am not proud of anything I did to you and it may be hard for you to believe but I do love you and want nothing but the best for you." I could not believe what I was hearing. "You love me? Do you even realize what you did? Have you ever verbally admitted what took place? I was forbidden to tell and you closed your eyes to the ugly truth. Tell me now what happened!! What exactly are you sorry for? You seem awfully quiet right now. Well let me help you." She stood up to leave and I jumped in her path. "Have a seat because for the first time you are going to hear the ugly truth. You will hear and hopefully understand the pain your child had to endure and then you tell me what man or love of a man was worth it? When you went to sleep at night, your husband left your bed and made his way to my bed. I can still smell his sweat to this day. His rough hands rubbing between my thighs and I, your child, was introduced to sex in its ugliest form. I was 10 years old for God's sake. It did not stop there. Your brother, my uncle, joined in and they both had their way with me. I cried night after night. When I tried to tell you, you dismissed me and made me feel like it had to be my fault. My life is forever scarred. I can't have a satisfying intimate relationship with my husband. I don't want children because of my fears. My life was ruined the first time he laid his hands on me and you wonder if I had anything to do with their deaths? Well no I didn't but please believe me when I tell you, I could have murdered both of them and felt no remorse." She just stared at me with tears running down her face. "And excuse me if your tears don't move me." She stood up and walked towards the front door and turned towards me. "I will continue to pray for you. I know you may never forgive me but I will pray that you find peace and happiness. I am truly sorry for my horrible decisions. I will not bother you anymore and if you ever." She did not continue. She left and I collapsed to the floor and I cried. I was crying because through all the pain she caused me, I still loved her. I did not want to love her. She was still my mother.

****

THIRTEEN

WHAT ABOUT LARRY

It was time for me to deal with Larry. Larry was extremely clever and I had to be very careful. Crystal called and wanted me to stop over for dinner. I checked with David and he was going to his father's once again. Looks like his father was not doing very well. I offered to go with him and he insisted that I go to dinner with Crystal and enjoy myself. I got to Crystal's place around six o'clock. She was pouring us a glass of wine. "I wanted to know if you were ready to tell me the rest of your story, specifically about Larry. I know it is difficult so if you are not ready, just let me know." "No that is ok, because actually talking about it is helpful.

While trying to run from Felix and Calvin, I ran into Larry. I endure the molestation from Felix and Calvin for six years. I felt so used up by the time I turned sixteen. When I turned sixteen, I decided I was running away from home. I ran away and ran into the arms of Larry. I was sixteen with no money, no job and basically nowhere to stay. I stole $140 from Felix and that was all I had. I rode the train into the city. I was walking the down 42nd street and that is where Larry spotted me. He was smooth and slick. He knew I was a runaway and slowly lured me in. Before I knew it, he was offering to let me stay with him and he was going to hook me up with a job. I was so naïve. Turns out that Larry was a pimp. The first couple of days he was so nice and generous. He bought me some clothes, fed me and gave me some money. Not once did I stop and think why would this man do all of this for a perfect stranger. On the fourth night with Larry he brutally raped me. After he raped me, he beat me up. He beat me so bad that I was no use to him for several weeks. After I healed up from the beating, he peddled me off to different men for money. Here I was again being abused. Then I started to wonder was there something wrong with me and was this all my fault. Larry would beat me regularly. As he put it, it was his way of keeping me in check. He beat me so bad one time that I could not see out of either of my eyes because they were swollen so bad. After two years Larry got arrested and I went back home because I had no place to go. After Larry got out of prison he decided to go straight. Even though he went straight he still had a nasty disposition. I would occasionally see him around town and he would look at me and stick out his tongue and lick his lips. He was a nasty monster. When I went back home I was eighteen and Felix did not bother me. I only stayed there until I was able to get a job and save up some money." Crystal was speechless. She was crying. "I wish there was something I could have done to help you. You have a testimony because look at where you are today. You should come to church with me on Sunday. You need to give God some praise for how he has turned your life around." What was it with everyone trying to get me into a church? First it was David and now Crystal. "Crystal I will take you up on your offer another time because this Sunday David and I are speeding some time together." Church was the last thing on my mind. I could not go to church because of what I was planning to do. Larry had to pay and I wanted to collect that payment. We had dinner and we talked some more. I left around ten and went home.

The following day I was trying to figure out how I was going to get Larry alone. This would be tricky because he would suspect something if I asked to see him. I could pay him a surprise visit but would he let me in his house. My only option was a surprise visit and hopefully he would let me in. I just needed to get in and close enough to stick him with the syringe. Tomorrow I would make him pay. Tomorrow I can bury my final monster. I was not sure how I would feel when it was done but I had to do this.

That night when David got home we spent some time together. But he seemed to be somewhere else. He was there with me physically but not mentally. I thought it must have been his father. David was very close with his father and with not being in the best of health it was probably taking a toll on David. There was no love making. He just held me in his arms until I feel asleep. I woke in the middle of the night drench in sweat and shaking because I had a terrible dream. I was in a building running from someone and I was covered in blood. I just kept running and he got closer and closer. David rolled over and asked if I were ok. "Just a bad dream. You go back to sleep." I knew the nightmare was because of Larry.

The following morning I was sleep when David got up. He was downstairs cooking but I did not get out of bed. He yelled, "Hey boo, are you awake? Do you want something to eat? I did not have the energy to yell, so I got up and went to the kitchen. "No I do not want anything to eat. I am not hungry and I am going to lazy around the house and go out to run some errands later." I went back to the bedroom and laid back down. After David left for work, I took a shower and prepared to go to Larry's apartment. I was not sure he would be home but I was going to try. I left the house at 11 am and headed to Larry's apartment. I was extremely nervous but I was determined. When I pulled up in front of Larry's apartment, I noticed his car parked out front and my nerves got worse. Part of my fear was I remembered just how badly he would beat me when he lost his temper. I knew if I was not careful and he caught wind of what I was trying to do, he would kill me. I made my way up to his apartment. His door was slightly ajar. This had a familiar feel to it and I did not like what I was thinking. I knocked on the door and yelled hello. There was no answer but suddenly I heard a very faint moan. As I stood there, my first thought was just get out of here because you don't want to know what is or who is inside that apartment moaning. But the need to know outweighed my common sense. I entered the apartment and closed the door behind me. I walked in the direction of the moaning and lying on the kitchen floor with blood all over was Larry. He was not dead but it looked like it was a matter time. Blood was everywhere and he had started to bleed from the mouth. I stood there for a few moments just staring at him. Then I got a folding chair that was in the corner by the refrigerator and sat right next to his body. "Hey Larry, you look like you are in pretty bad shape. Who did this to you. No don't answer, save your energy. I am pretty sure you deserved this. Probably hurt some young girl and this was your payback. Unfortunately, I can't muster up any sympathy for you, but I am going to take this opportunity to get some things off my chest and I guess you have no choice but to hear me, unless your flame is extinguished before I finish." I saw a single tear drop from his eye as he gasps for air. "Wow what does that tear represent? Is it remorse? Is it pain? What are you feeling right now? I don't think it is remorse. You never showed an ounce of compassion so I am not sure you are remorseful in any way. I will tell you what I am feeling right now. I am feeling fed up and ready to see you suffer. You will never understand or comprehend the changes that took place in my life. You hurt me so deep, both physically and mentally. You stole my youth and womanhood from me. I can't enjoy intimacy with my husband. I don't think you understand or even care. I am taking pleasure in watching you suffer. I am hoping that your pain is 10 times the pain you inflicted on me." As he was gasping for air, I could faintly hear him cry for help. "That is the same thing I did, I cried for help so many times and no one came to my aid. You did not care." His eyes slowly closed and the life slipped out of him. He was dead. I sat there for a few moments trying to comprehend what I was feeling. I waited for this moment and I honestly felt nothing. I was not sure how I was supposed to feel but I was sure of one thing; Felix, Calvin or Larry would not be able to hurt another little girl or young woman. Then it suddenly dawned on me that all three men that I intended on killing were dead. Someone beat me to the punch but who and why. I got up and placed the chair back where I found it. I took a handkerchief from my purse and wipe the chair clean of fingerprints and left the apartment. When I got in the car something happened that I did not expect, I felt an overwhelming urge to cry. I tried to fight back the tears but to no avail. At that moment, I could not understand my feelings. I should not be crying, I couldn't stop crying. I wanted the tears to stop flowing.

FOURTEEN

****

NO CHANGE

When I got home I took a shower and put on a sexy outfit that David bought for me last year. I cooked a roast with vegetables and mash potatoes. I pulled out a bottle of Merlot and lit some candles to set the mood. It was time to allow myself to be intimate with my husband and enjoy it. I wanted everything to be perfect. David deserved this and so much more. I was ready to be his wife for the first time. When David got home, he was speechless. "Oh, my I must have died and gone to heaven. What did I do to deserve this?" He pulled me into his arms and kissed me softly and gently. "How about we skip dinner and go straight to desert?"

I felt so empowered. "No I slaved over that stove to make you a meal fit for a king. So, we shall eat dinner first." While we ate dinner, David could not take his off me. It was as if he was seeing me for the first time. "Everything is so good. I love you Mrs. Matthews." When dinner was finished, we took our glasses of wine and went into the bedroom. We sat on the bed and David began to kiss and caress me and suddenly I felt like Roxanne at the age of thirteen again. I wanted to die at that very moment. I wanted him to stop touching me. All three demons, dead and still I suffer. I faked my way through the sex and when David fell asleep, I turned over and cried myself to sleep.

The following morning David was getting dressed and he turned to me, "Was something wrong last night? You seem a little distance when we were making love." He usually did not notice my distant behavior when we were making love. "I think that wine got me a little sick and I didn't want to say anything because I did not want to spoil our evening. I promise I will make it up to you." He came over and kissed me on the forehead. "No need to make up anything. You are wonderful even when you are feeling a little under the weather." I wanted things to change and I thought seeing the demons dead would be what I needed. I guess maybe I should try the traditional path like a shrink or God. I wanted things to change and I needed them to change. David left for work and I decided I was going to just lay around the house. My phone started vibrating, which was an indication that I had a message. I went to check my phone and it was a message from my mother. She was checking to see if I heard about Larry and did I want to talk. My mother knew about some of what went on with Larry. I did not bother to answer and I deleted the message. About 30 minutes later my phone rang and it was her again. I snatched up my phone and answered it. "What do you want? I am not in the mood to deal with you today." She was not one to give up easily. I guess I got that from her. "Roxanne something is going on and I am not calling to accuse you.

Don't you find it strange that in a short span, all three men that abused you are dead. Something is not right." I did not want to have this conversation right now but she was persistent. "Wow, you just admitted that I was abused on your watch. So, tell me this, why should I care about the deaths of my molesters?" She had an answer for everything. "Because despite all of your hurt and pain, you know that vengeance is mine sayeth the Lord. Vengeance will not heal the brokenness. That healing comes from God." I felt the rage rising. "Where was God when I was being repeatedly raped and beaten? Where was God when you knew that your husband left your bed to go and get in bed with your daughter? I guess it is wonderful that you have God now and that might work for you but for me right now I am not sure what works. Just leave me alone please." I hung up the phone. I was upset but it was not so much about my mother. I was more upset because I was feeling bad about the death of the demons. I was wondering how could I possibly have an ounce of concern about them. I felt like my sanity was slipping away. I was fighting the urge to be compassionate. After all I had endured, I was not suppose to have room for compassion. Then I started to focus on who could have possibly killed all 3 of these men. Were my demons someone else's demons?

FIFTEEN

I AM SORRY

I was trying to get my life back to normal. I decided I might go back to work. Sitting around the house was not working for me. Today was Sunday and I promised David I would go to church. There was a struggle going on inside of me. Yes, I felt like I needed to go to church but I also felt guilty sitting in God's house after the things I plotted even though I was not the one to carry them out. When we got home from church, David said he needed to go and take care of some things for his dad and he would be home latter tonight. An hour later my doorbell rang. I looked out the peephole and there was a young lady standing there. I opened the door. "May I help you?" She smiled. "Hi my name is Carmen Dyson." Dyson? Could this be Larry's wife? And if it was, why the hell was she standing on my doorstep. "Larry Dyson is my father. I was wondering if I could speak with you for a moment." I asked her to come in. The invite into my house was out of curiosity more than anything. We went into the living room. "I am not sure if you heard but my father was murdered." I told her that I heard about it on the news. "Well I am here because I have a letter that my father asked me to give to you if anything ever happened to him." I was caught off guard. "Your father talked to you about me?" I was shocked that he would mention me to his daughter. "Not really. He just told me that he had to make some things right and that he did some things that he was not proud of and he wanted to make amends. My father was not a perfect man but I loved him. I am not sure what he did to you or how he hurt you but it was very important to him that you get this letter. I can't ask you to forgive him but I can tell you that he changed his life for the better and for that I was proud of him. My father did some things that I found hard to forgive but he was my father and I had to believe in him" When she said that I thought about his menacing phone call. Did he really change? I did not get that impression from the phone call. I took the letter from her. "Thank you and I am so sorry for your loss." As she stood to leave, I had the urge to hug her and I did. With a father like Larry there was no telling what type of abuse she had to live with as a child. When she left, I read the letter.

Roxanne I don't know where to start but I guess I will just start with I am sorry. I know saying sorry does not make up for all the horrible things that I did to you. I know that you may never forgive me but I must say this for my salvation. I do not want to die without repenting. I need to get right with God so I am not condemned to hell.

At that point I stopped reading. I could not believe what I was reading. He was concerned about himself and there was not sincerity to this letter. Why would I expect anything different? I did not have the energy to get angry. Larry is now a distant memory. Now I needed to think about healing Roxanne. I needed to get my head right so I could be the wife that David deserved. It was time. It was 11 pm and David was not home. At first, I did not worry much but when I called and he did not answer I became a little worried. I had a restless sleep because David did not come home at all. This was so out of character for David. I decide to call David's father. I got no answer. Now my worry became panic. David's mother and father had been separated for many years but I thought she might have heard something from David. "Hi Paulette, this is Roxanne. I was just wondering have you heard from David?" "No sweetheart I have not heard from him. You know David and I were close but he let his father fill his head with junk." I did not want to hear this regurgitated conversation. "Well do you know if his father is ok?" There was a moment of silence. "What are you talking about? David father died about 2 months ago." I could not catch my breath. I just hung up the phone and sat on the edge of my bed in disbelief. David had been lying to me. His father was dead. How could he not tell me that his father was dead and why would he let me believe he was still alive. And most of all, where was he? None of this made sense. Was he having an affair? But to let me think your father was alive just to cover up an affair seemed extreme. I felt like my world was crashing down around me. There were no men in my life that I could truly trust and believe it. I needed answers but I did not know where to find David. My phone rang and of course it was my mother calling at a time I just did not want to deal with her. I ignored the call but she continued to call until I finally picked up the phone. "Can't you take a hint? If I don't pick up the phone, that means I do not want to talk. Leave me alone." "Roxanne I need to talk to you about David." What did she know about David? "What about David?" She hesitated, "You need to drive out to Rikers Island and ask to speak to him. Visiting hours tomorrow are from 1pm to 9pm. Go see your husband." Before I could respond she hung up the phone. Was I in the twilight zone because my world just flipped upside down. Why would David be in Rikers Island? David doesn't even have a parking ticket. I needed answers now so I called my mother back. She would not answer her phone. When do I get of this roller coaster?

SIXTEEN

****

A HUSBAND'S LOVE

The following morning I was up early and I did not sleep most of the night. I was nervous and did not know what to expect. I did know that my life was changed forever. The ride to Rikers Island seemed like the longest ride I have ever taken. I checked in and went to visitors' area. I still had no idea why my husband was being detained at Rikers Island. I did not notice my own leg shaking while sitting and waiting to see David. I was so scared and nervous. I was finally called and when they brought David out he had on an orange jumpsuit with chains around his ankles and he was handcuff. This was serious. They uncuffed his hands and a glass window separated us. Our only means of communication was a telephone. An officer stood right behind him as if he was going to get up and walk out the door. The tears started streaming down my face. I picked up the phone and he did the same. "What is going on? Why are you in here?"

Before he answered I already knew. It finally dawned on me. "David, it was you." He lowered his head because he could not look me in the eyes. "When I started reading your journal, I learned so much about you that you never told me. I often wondered why you would flinch at my touch or how you pretended to be so into our lovemaking. At first I thought it was me. I thought that I was not man enough for you and I thought I would find the answers in your journal. I found that answers alright but not the answers that I thought. I understood and at the same time I became so angry at what these men did to you. I could not approach you because I felt I betrayed you trust by reading your personal journal. Only thing I could do was let you know that I was there for you any time you needed to talk. Then your writings took on a darker tone and your anger started to manifest. Revenge was your obsession and I knew if you carried out your plan for revenge I would lose you forever. You will never know how much I love you. I was willing to give up my life for you. I figure I could get revenge for you and save you from a prison cell. I could not bear seeing you in prison after all you have endured in your life. You deserve some peace." I was heartbroken. "But how can I have peace without you. I am so sorry that this has happened." He finally raised his head and looked me in the eyes. "Don't be sorry because this was my choice and I have to live with it. I just want you to get the help you need and start being happy again. Try to forget about me and live your life." The guard stepped forward and said we had five minutes. "David, you are my husband and I will never forget about you. I will make sure you have the best lawyers in the world and we will beat this somehow." He looked at me with such hopelessness. "I will not let you go into debt trying to defend me. I am guilty 3 counts of first degree murder. Life in prison with no possibility of parole. I killed three men. Roxanne, I have accepted responsibility for my crimes and I hope you find it in your heart to forgive me and most of all forgive your mother. She has changed" The tears were a steading flow by now. "I have nothing to forgive you for. I know why you did what you did and I still love you and I will still stand by you." The guard stated that I time was up. As he was led away it was as if someone was twisting a knife in my heart. When I left the prison, it was as if I was in a daze. I drove straight to my mother's house. She opened the door and I fell into her arms. For the first time, I needed my mother and I was willing to try to mend this relationship. We went into the house to talk. "I am not sure that I will ever forget what you did but I am willing to try and work on our relation. I see what Christ has done in your life and you are a changed person. We will have to start slow because I have to work on me first. What my husband did is not right but I love him and I will stay in contact with him. I just need help getting my head straight." She went to a drawer and pulled out a box and handed it to me. "I have been waiting to give this to you." I took the box and opened it. There was a beautiful bible in the box. "Try God for a change. Pray and cry out to the Lord. He has been my healer and comforter. I never thought I could get over my past but with the help of God I am a new person. His grace is sufficient." I stood up to leave. "I won't make any promises but I will try. It is hard for me because I still wonder how God could allow those things to happen to me?" She looked at me and smiled, "Ask him"

When I got home it was so lonely in the house but I had to redesign my life and I started with going to church that Sunday and made an appointment with the Pastor and a psychologist to start counseling. I was determined to get my life on the right track. I visited David once a week. He fought me at first but I think he appreciated me. When he was moved upstate to serve his life sentence I continued to go and see him. On our visits, we would read the bible and I would pray with him. As usual Crystal was my rock. She was there for me every step of the way. It was a long journey back. My final journey was forgiving the three men who caused me so much pain. I would never forget but I did need to forgive so I could get my life back. Forgiveness was not for Felix, Calvin or Larry sake. It was meant to give me peace and freedom.

ABOUT THE AUTHOR

Born and raised in Brooklyn, New York, Shannon Spruill has a passion for reading and a very creative imagination. She always had a vision of becoming an author. Shannon graduated Suma Cum Laude from Bryant and Stratton College with a Bachelor's degree in Business Administration and a Master's degree in Computer Information Systems from Boston University. She has worked in the computer technology field for over 15 years and is a modern-day gadget geek. Looking for a new road to travel Shannon decided to pursue her lifelong desire to write her first book and has begun to embark upon this journey. Her desire has always been to write fiction but she felt she had a story to tell.

Shannon's first book was released December 1, 2010. "My Reflection in the Mirror" is a look at some personal demons that she had to overcome. She hopes by telling her story she can inspire and empower other women.

October 4, 2013 Shannon lost her son Brian in an automobile accident. This was a devastating tragedy but instead of sinking into a dark place, Shannon grieved and rose up with the help of God and began helping other parents that have lost a child. With the help of her husband, Shannon started a support group for parents, grandparents and siblings who have lost a child.

It continues to be a long journey but with her deep spiritual conviction and relationship with God, Shannon has learned how to overcome the obstacles in her life. She credits everything in her life and who she is today to God.

www.ingramcontent.com/pod-product-compliance
Lightning Source LLC
Chambersburg PA
CBHW060129260626
47160CB00005B/2055